A long time ago, there was a tortoise who was very chatty. The tortoise lived next to a lake. He went there every morning to have a drink, and to chat to the animals who swam there.

“Good morning, Geese! Are you well, Heron? What fine weather we are having, Crane! Ooh, Ducks, Did I tell you about the time I...”

The tortoise chatted all the time. In fact, he found it quite hard to keep his mouth shut! Despite this, the geese and the tortoise were good friends.

Then the rain stopped falling. There was no rain for weeks and weeks. The rivers dried up. Then the ponds dried up. Then the lake where the tortoise and his friends lived dried up, too.

"Whatever shall we do?" wailed the tortoise. "It is terrible! We cannot drink or swim here!"

"We are all going," said the crane. "I myself am going to a deep pond fifty miles west of here."

"Fifty miles!" exclaimed the tortoise. "That is fifty weeks' trekking for me. I will never make it!"

“We are going to a wide river,” said the ducks. “It is just twenty miles south as the duck flies.”

“But that is too far as well!” complained the tortoise.

“I am going to a lake in the mountains. It is only five miles from here,” said the heron.

“Uphill? I cannot trek up a steep mountain on these little legs!” wailed the tortoise.

“We are going to the lake in the mountains as well,” said the geese.

“I can carry you if you like,” said one of the geese. “Can you ride on my back?”

The tortoise tried to get on the goose's back, but her feathers were too smooth and he kept falling off.

"Perhaps we can carry you together with the help of this," said the geese, pointing to a long stick.

The geese bit onto the ends of the stick, and told the tortoise to do the same. Then they lifted him off the ground.

"This is fantastic!" shouted the tortoise, and he promptly fell to the ground.

"You will need to keep your mouth closed around the stick until we get to the mountain lake," explained the geese.

So the tortoise held on, and off they went.

As they crossed a dried-up river, some animals giggled and pointed at the tortoise.

“He looks so silly up there,” said a leopard.

“He is funny,” chortled a tiger.

The tortoise was so angry that he opened his mouth to shout at them. As he did so, he lost his grip on the stick, and fell!

"Argh!" he yelled.

The tortoise landed upside down in a tree. On seeing this, even his friends chuckled and pointed at him.

“You do look funny!” they said.

The tortoise felt so silly that he never spoke again for the rest of his life. As the geese chatted on and on, the tortoise just listened!